# The Freaky Joe Club

Other books by P. J. McMahon

# The Freaky Joe Club

Illustrated by
John Manders

# The Freaky Joe Club

## Secret File #5:

## The Mystery of the Disappearing Dinosaurs

by
P. J. McMahon

ALADDIN PAPERBACKS
New York  London  Toronto  Sydney

To the one, the only UB,
my friend Brian McCarthy
— P. J. M.

❧ALADDIN PAPERBACKS
An imprint of Simon & Schuster Children's Publishing Division
1230 Avenue of the Americas, New York, NY 10020
Text copyright © 2005 by Patricia McMahon
Illustrations copyright © 2005 by John Manders
All rights reserved, including the right of reproduction in whole or in part in any form.
ALADDIN PAPERBACKS and colophon are trademarks of Simon & Schuster, Inc.
Designed by Lisa Vega
The text of this book was set in 14-point Minion.
Manufactured in the United States of America
First Aladdin Paperbacks edition August 2005
10  9  8  7  6  5  4  3  2  1
Library of Congress Control Number 2005920611
ISBN 1-4169-0049-7

# Table of Contents

## Chapter One

# Mystery Man Dodges Alien Ships

Yes, it is a great honor, no doubt about it, to be asked to form a chapter of the Freaky Joe Club. To be handed the red book with the bicycle chain wrapped around it, to be told of Freaky Joe, of how the club came to be. It's a big deal all right, but sometimes, well, sometimes it can feel like . . . like . . . well, okay . . . like homework.

I mean, it wasn't very long ago I wrote down the tale of the Freaky Joe Club and the Case of the Psychic Hamster. I thought we were smart, cool, crime-solving guys. We had done a good job and now we could settle into school. Relax. Read a good mystery or two. I didn't think that in a very short time I would have to tell of another mystery. A tale of strange creatures. And strange songs. Oh, and blue hair . . .

"I've done it!" I announce to The Beast and The Hamster. "I've finished the newest Remington Reedmarsh." I do a small Finished Book End Zone dance.

Riley thumps her tail to show she is happy for me. Bob the Hamster, the newest member of the Freaky Joe Club crime-solving team, gives me a hamster salute.

"Okay, I am definitely the mystery-reading champion," I tell my brave companions. "And now I need something new to read."

I head over to the bookshelf in The Secret Place. Since it's Saturday, I'll get a good start on the book before I go back to school Monday.

Except . . .

"Oh no!" I cry out.

Riley lifts her head this time. She growls low.

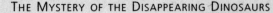

Bob starts karate-chopping the air. "I have no more books to read! A crisis!"

Riley and Bob look confused. I rush out the door and to the house.

I find my mom upstairs in the room where we used to watch TV, and where now she paints her paintings. Big paintings.

3

This one is of a giant orange chair.

"Mom, I have an emergency. I need to go to Big Blue."

"What's an emergency?" says a voice from under a nearby table.

"An emergency is when I have no new books to read," I explain to my little sister, Bella.

"I'll tell you a story if you want," the voice promises. "It will be about a unicorn named Stella, and her best friends, Jimmy and Jeff."

"Thanks, but can you tell me when I get home? From the bookstore?" I say, turning to my mom. Who is covered in orange and yellow paint.

"You can go," she tells me. "*If* you wear a helmet, and stay on the sidewalk, and cross the street only on a green light, and call me when you get there, and again just before you leave."

"I promise. And I will avoid warriors from other planets." I cross my heart.

"Boys who make fun of their mother will be

told to stay at home, empty the dishwasher, and watch *The Sweetest Unicorn Movie* with their sister." My mom adds one green stripe to the orange chair.

"Just call me Polite Guy," I yell as I head out the door.

Riding alone through the streets of our neighborhood, I see no alien ships about to fire death rays. The only thing I see is the Ship's Cove Security truck parked by the entrance. Bubba Butowski, our ace security guard, sits behind the wheel. There are no dogs in the back of the truck, or sitting in the truck. Just Bubba sitting there reading a newspaper. And shaking his head.

"Hey hey, Bubba," I call out.

Bubba doesn't look up.

I can't stop to see why. I fly on. I am on a mission.

• • • •

The bells on the door ring as I head into the Big Blue Bookstore. Which most of us call Big Blue for short. And which isn't very big, but is definitely blue. Blue walls, blue words written on the walls, oh, and blue hair on the owner.

"Hey hey, Conor, how's the guy?" Miz Barnes leans down from high up on a ladder. She stacks books on top of books that are on top of the bookcase filled with books.

You gotta love this store. At least if you love books.

I do.

6

"Hey hey. Just picking up a new book." I head back toward the mystery section. At least I try to. But I can't get there. The bookstore is not the bookstore. All the book-covered tables are pushed to the sides. The coffee tray, and more important, the cookies, are gone. There's a platform up front, blocking the mystery section. Coach Pablo from the swim team is here setting up chairs. Lots of chairs.

"Come on, let's finish up." Miz Barnes lifts a basket filled with gray hippopotamuses wearing green and yellow skirts or hats. Actually, *hippopotami* is the right word, says *Animals of the World, Volume I.* Or as Bella would say, "That's not a hippopotamus, that's George."

"You will never get everyone in here, I swear," Pablo says as he moves the large red clock that holds alphabet books.

"Oh we will, we will." Miz Barnes runs her hands through her hair, making it stand straight up in the air. This usually means she's worried about something. I could say I know this because I am a great detective, but actually, she's one of my mom's two best friends. So I've seen her do this before.

"A customer is here who wants to get to the mystery section," I announce.

"Tell that customer to use his big brain to find a way there," Miz Barnes calls from the back room.

I climb up on the platform. I wonder where Miz Barnes got this? Looking out at the store from up here, I feel like I should give a speech. Like Remington Reedmarsh telling all the lemurs to be brave before they head into battle against the Terrible Tyrant Tyler. What's that I see out there, behind the cash register? A marsupial of enormous size? "Be brave!" I call out, banging my sword against my shield. "We are noble warriors, and our cause is a mighty and righteous one."

"I'm feeling brave," Miz Barnes answers.

I'm feeling like a doofus of enormous size.

"Great speech, little dude," Pablo tells me. "Where did you learn to talk like that?"

"He reads," Miz Barnes tells Pablo. "Books. The things on the shelves in this store."

"Cool. But where are you going to put the TV guys?" Pablo asks.

"Shhh," Miz Barnes says.

"TV?" I ask.

"Mystery section." She points.

Mystery section? How about a mystery bookstore! What's going on here?

"The new Sir Chester is here," Miz Barnes tells me. "Pablo, we need to finish pronto." She points to the large pile of chairs.

Climbing down the other side of the platform, I run my finger down the books on the mystery shelf till I find the right one. Pulling it from the shelf, I read:

**Sir Chester the Clever and the Strange Dragon Mystery: Being the Eighth Episode in the Adventures of Sir Chester and His Brave Squire, Chuck**

Looking at the picture on the cover, I laugh. That would be a strange dragon, all right! I have got to get home to read this. I leap onto the platform, ready to pay, ready to read.

"I think TV cameras can go here," Miz Barnes is telling Pablo as I rush up.

"TV cameras?" I ask.

"It's nothing," says Miz Barnes.

"It's something," I answer, pointing at the store.

"He's a smart little dude," Pablo says.

"Yes, I know," Miz Barnes says. "A real Mystery Man."

"I need to buy this—I have got to read about that." I show her the strange dragon.

"I'll ring you up, while you call your mom to say you're heading home. Pablo, put the 'Closed' sign in the window." Miz Barnes's hair is not just sticking up, it's pointing out where the sky is, to anyone who might be confused.

I call. I pay. I hop on my bicycle.

Riding home I wonder how Sir Chester has found such a strange dragon. And what is going on at the Big Blue Bookstore? Sounds to me like I have come home with not one, but two mysteries. Good thing I am Mystery Man.

## Chapter Two

# And the Question Is?

"Gadzooks, my good squire Chuck! What can this beast be? I know not a dragon that looks like this."

"Then we must be sure he is not a dragon," Chuck says. "For a dragon looks like a dragon. And this looks like . . ."

"Like what, my good Chuck, like what?" Sir Chester waves his lance around.

"I'm thinking, I'm thinking!" Chuck yells.

Just then, a dreadful noise fills the air.

"Yo-de-lay-hee-oh! Yo-de-lay-hee-oh!" A strange creature indeed flies through the door of The Secret Place, crying out in an odd and terrible voice. Wearing a large, strange something on his head.

"How do you like my hat and my singing, pardner?"

Ah, a large and strange hat.

I need a minute before I can tell Jack just what I think of the horrible noise he is making, and the gigantic cowboy hat that is covering all of his head and half of his face.

But Riley doesn't. The Beast jumps to her four doggie feet. She runs to the door. And leaps onto Jack.

"Noooooo, Riley! Not my hat!" Jack cries as he goes down. Which sounds better than the noise he was making.

Riley leaves his hat alone, but licks and licks his face.

"Capital G, capital R, capital O, capital S, capital S!" Jack yells.

"Spelling while being kissed by a dog is an impressive skill," I tell Jack. Freaky Joe's Rule Number Four: Always Be Encouraging.

"Thank you for telling me something nice before I'm eaten alive by a dog."

"She just wants to make sure you're okay. You sounded terrible when you came through the door," I tell him.

"Riley girl! Good dog for attacking that mean varmint there." Riley quickly leaves Jack, running to greet Timmy as he comes in the door. I could be wrong, but he seems to be covered in large brown paper bags.

"Timmy, what are you wearing?" I ask Timmy.

"Do you want a treat, Riley girl?" Timmy asks Riley.

"I'm supposed to sound terrible—don't you get it?" Jack asks me.

"What am I wearing? Can't you tell?" Timmy asks.

"Would I ask you if I could tell?" I ask.

"Why is no one listening to me?" Jack asks.

Riley runs around and around in a circle in

front of Timmy. Which is doggie talk for "Where's the treat?"

"What's wrong, girl?" Timmy asks.

"Why are we all talking in questions?" I ask.

"Can't you see I'm dressed in buckskin clothes for riding the range?" Timmy turns round and round like Riley.

"Huh?" Jack says.

"Maybe we're being haunted?" Timmy suggests.

"Maybe we're not?" I say.

"Maybe I am really the superhero Question Man?" Jack begins to fly around the room. Well, he pretends to fly. With the very large cowboy hat covering his face, he trips over the beanbag chair.

"What superpower does Question Man have?" Timmy asks. "Does he have the amazing ability to fall over chairs?"

"Does he have the amazing ability to attack Grocery Bag Man?" Jack flies across the room, tackling Timmy.

"Who will save me, who will save me?" Timmy calls out.

Riley will. She leaps to his rescue.

"Noooooooooo!" Jack calls as Riley squishes him flat.

Finally. The question spell is broken.

*Bang.* The door flies open. Bella stands at the door, wearing a pink cowgirl hat, a pink cowgirl skirt, a white shirt with pink fringe, and pink cowboy boots.

With his tremendous mystery skills, Mystery Man realizes everyone is dressing up for a reason.

"Is this your Halloween costume?" I ask Bella.

"Don't be silly, Conor," Bella says as she does a handstand.

But he does not yet know the reason.

"Mom wants to know when you're coming," she says. "She says to say you'll be late for dinner, and Billy Bob Big Business."

Aha. Billy Bob. TV. Timmy and Jack coming over. Blame it on Sir Chester, but I forgot. Now big hats and grocery bags make sense.

"Coming through, coming through!" Jack jumps up fast enough to knock Riley off. Pulling his hat down low, he quickly runs into the wall.

"Grocery Bag Man defeats Question Man," Timmy yells as he runs out the door.

I wonder if I should tell him he left a piece of his cowboy pants on the floor.

I won't have to. Riley runs out with it in her mouth.

Bella runs after him yelling,

"Business! Business!"

I wonder if I should tell her the right word.

Jack runs out in the wrong direction.

I wonder if I should declare tonight Do Not Even Try to Solve a Mystery Night. My fellow detectives are blind, or covered in brown paper, and I forgot about tonight's big TV show.

"I'll get there first," Jack yells as he heads toward the pool gate.

I wonder if I can catch him before he hits the fence.

"Owww!"

That would be a no. But what was that thought that just ran across my brain? TV? TV show? TV cameras? Pablo said it. "I think the TV cameras should go here."

What TV cameras? Why are they coming to Big Blue? So many questions that need answers.

"What's wrong? I can't move!" Jack cries out.

Questions such as "How am I going to get Jack out of the fence?"

# Chapter Three
## That's Billy Bob Bidness, Boys

"Okay, special delivery of famous homemade pizza," Mom announces. She balances two big trays on her hands. "But before you fill your mouths with pepperoni, tell me what is the big deal?"

"It's the final show of *Did You Hear That?*" I tell her.

"Tonight they're going to pick the winner," Jack adds.

"They've been searching for the worst singer in America," Timmy explains.

"This is a joke, right?" my mom asks.

"No joke," I promise.

"We want Billy Bob Bidness to win," Jack goes on. "So we're dressing like cowboys to cheer him on."

"'Cause he's a Texan," Timmy explains. "See, these are my buckskin clothes for riding the range."

"Clearly," Mom says.

"I'm a cowgirl," Bella reminds her.

"Since all Texans are cowboys or cowgirls," Mom asks, "why don't you three go down and muck out the stables for me?"

"What stables?" Jack asks.

"What's muck?" Timmy asks. "Does it taste good?"

"Quiet! It's starting." I lean over and turn up the sound.

"Welcome, America," says a man in a tuxedo, "to the great and grand finale of *Did You Hear That?* Tonight we will know once and for all just who is the worst singer in our fair land."

Lights swirl. The audience claps and cheers.

The first contestant, Harriet Hatzy, comes out wearing a dress that looks an awful lot like a hot-air balloon. Throwing her head back so far it looks like she might end up singing to the ceiling, she opens her mouth wide. And hollers. A long, loud, sad, bad song about the day Tulip, her goat, ran off, leaving her all sad and lonesome.

"Would you call that the worst?" Timmy says. "I wouldn't."

"Maybe Tulip is lost inside her dress?" Bella suggests.

"This is a joke, right?" my mom asks.

"Shhh, here he comes," Jack insists.

The announcer's voice shouts out, "Let's hear it for finalist number two, Billy Bob Bidness!"

"Go, Billy Bob!" All the cowboys, cowgirls, and grocery bag people jump up and down.

Billy Bob takes the stage wearing a big, tall cowboy hat; big, tall cowboy boots; and a cowboy shirt with long fringe. He opens his mouth.

"Yo-de-lay-hee, yo-de-lay-hee, yo-de-lay-hee-oh!" he howls, or yodels, loudly. And badly.

Bella jumps out of her chair and hides behind Mom.

"Isn't that awful?" my mom says.

"Let's hope so," Jack says. "I want him to win."

Billy Bob commences to sing.

"I love my truck!
Oh, she brings me luck,
Yup, she cost me twenty buck
from a guy named Chuck,
who drove it through the muck,
oh, a-hunting for some duck.
Yo-de-lay-hee, yo-de-lay-hee,
yo-de-lay-hee-oh!"

"We know that guy Chuck, don't we, Conor? He's in your books," Bella points out.

"I think we're the winners," Jack says.

"This is a joke, right?" my mom asks.

The announcer reminds everyone that this

show is sponsored by the Doesn't That Smell Clean? Company. And that the company will give the winner a ten-year supply of Doesn't That Smell Clean? cleaning products, as well as sponsor a special event in the winner's honor.

Then the lights flash, sirens sound, an envelope is delivered. The announcer calls out the name:

"Billy Bob Bidness!"

"Yes!" Jack shouts, pumping his fist into the air.

"This is a joke, yes?" my mom asks.

Billy Bob wipes tears from his eyes. He waves at the camera and yells, "Go, Texas!"

"Go, Billy Bob!" we yell. I have no idea why I did that.

"Are you ready, Houston?" he shouts into the microphone. "'Cause I'm a-coming your way."

"Houston?" Jack asks.

"We live here," Timmy tells him.

"That's right," the announcer says. "Billy Bob Bidness is going home to Texas for his special prize. Which Billy Bob and the Doesn't That Smell Clean? Company promise will be a whole corral full of fun."

"So y'all get ready." Billy Bob gets up close to the camera. "I'll see everyone at the Big Blue Bookstore on Tuesday night. And I'll fill you in on all the fun we're a-fixing to have."

"The Big Blue Bookstore!" I shout.

"Our bookstore!" Bella says.

"Fun, we're going to have fun," Jack says.

"Big Blue?" Mom looks confused. "Valerie didn't tell me."

"She was setting up for something big today," I tell her.

"I better go call her and Molly," Mom says, heading out the door.

"I say we'd better do the Billy Bob Hula!" Timmy calls out.

None of us knows what that is. But we do it just the same.

## Chapter Four

# Such a Nice, Happy Family

"Whoa, look at that!" Jack shouts.

My mom pulls our truck up to the Big Blue Bookstore.

"I guess a lot of people like singing that hurts your ears," Bella says.

"A whole lotta people," Timmy agrees.

There are cars everywhere. And trucks. Even trucks with antennae on top, and names of TV stations on the side.

The TV people, I realize.

"Good thing I made this poster." Jack waves his roll of paper. "We'll get on TV for sure."

Jack has made a large banner saying SHIP'S COVE LOVES BILLY BOB. There are a lot of dancing horses on it. And Jack is not the best artist I know.

"Too bad I didn't wear my buckskins," Timmy says.

"Riley ate a lot of your buckskins," Bella says.

"Look, even Bubba's here!" Jack points. The Ship's Cove Security truck sits in a space near the store.

"Okay, kids, stick together," Mom says. "And I'll get us into this place."

"I didn't know you liked Billy Bob," Bella says.

"I like to know what's going on," she answers.

"We knew that, didn't we, guys?" Jack gives a big double wink, sticking one elbow out to the side.

"Are you trying to be a chicken today?" Bella looks confused.

"No, just discussing a little secret among other knowers of secrets." Jack gives the strange wink again.

"I don't know what that means," Bella admits.

"It means Jack is not a good person to tell a secret," I explain.

"There's Molly McGuire." Mom points.

"Come on, guys," Molly calls. "I've saved us a place."

"If he sings, I gotta run the other way," Mom informs me.

"If he yodels, I'll probably cry," Bella says.

The store is so packed there is hardly room to breathe. Pablo is lying across six chairs in the front.

"I gotta go work backstage, so these are all for you little dudes," he says. "Oh, and grown-ups with the little dudes."

"You should see the banner I've got," Jack tells him as he sticks it alongside his chair.

"Cool."

"Where's Valerie?" Mom asks.

"Miz Barnes is running around worrying," Pablo tells her.

"Miz Barnes doesn't know what to do with all these people," Miz Barnes says as she squishes her way up front. Her hair stands straight up on edge.

"Try selling them books," I suggest.

"Books? No one can get at them." She points around the room.

It is wall-to-wall bodies, grown-ups and kids. I wave at Bubba, who's standing by the wall with his arms crossed. He lifts a finger at me. But no smile.

He must hate to be here without a dog to keep him company, I guess.

A tall man with short hair and a short lady with tall yellow hair push their way to the front of the store. They are both wearing bright green shirts.

"Where is Miz Barnes? Miz Barnes?" they call out.

"Present." She waves at them.

The lady with tall yellow hair says, "I am Miss Evie Evan; I am in charge of Mr. Bidness for the Doesn't That Smell Clean? Company. This is Mr. G. Labanowski, our president." They both turn around. The backs of their shirts say DOESN'T THAT SMELL CLEAN?

"Well, great," Miz Barnes says. "I'm the owner of the bookstore, but there's no message on my shirt. As you can see we've had a great turnout."

"Yes, yes, fine, but how shall we bring Billy Bob into the store?" Miss Evie Evan asks.

"Can't Billy Bob walk?" Bella asks.

"In through this crowd?" Miss Evan sniffs.

"That would be the crowd of people who like him," Miz Barnes tells her. "I'll get Pablo to make a path up the middle."

"Or we could get Jack to do something gross," Timmy suggests. "That would clear a path."

"Yes, but would they come back?" asks Mr. G. Labanowski, president of the Doesn't That Smell Clean? Company.

Pablo sticks out his long, bony elbows, clearing a path. The crowd pushes. People start to stand on chairs. One gets knocked over, almost onto me.

"I got it, big buddy." Bubba leans over, grabbing the chair.

"No room for dogs, huh?" I tell him.

"No place for dogs," Bubba says.

"Hand me my poster," Jack says, jumping up and down.

"I can't get it, it's under the chair." I try to pull it out.

"All right, everyone, let's give a big Texas welcome to the worst singer in America!" Mr. G. Labanowski starts the clapping.

"I can't see him," Bella says.

"That's because it's a little hard to do," I point out as Billy Bob climbs up onto Miz Barnes' platform. Billy Bob looks fancy in his big, tall cowboy hat, and his tall cowboy boots with the Lone Star flag on them. But to be polite, that's the only thing tall about Billy Bob.

"Hoo-ah!" someone shouts.

"Hoo-ah back at you," Billy Bob says. "And I'm sending a great big howdy to all you good people here. It is sure an honor for me to be here tonight with all of you. And all the fine folks from the Doesn't That Smell Clean? Company."

Mr. G. Labanowski and Miss Evie Evans wave little, small waves and smile tiny, tight smiles.

"Who would have ever thought that this here humble good ol' boy could rise to the heights of fame singing about his good ol' truck?"

"Sing it, Billy Bob—sing the song," a voice shouts from the crowd.

"I get scared when you yodel," Bella calls loudly.

"Oh, maybe we'll get to some singing, but first I have some telling to do. You see, I won this here prize that says I get to do something special. And I'm choosing to do something for the good people of Texas, who are like family to me." At this Billy Bob pulls his hat off and holds it over his heart for a moment.

"Aww," murmurs the crowd.

"Oh, for goodness' sake," mutters my mom.

"You see, I knew I had to come home to share this prize. For I wouldn't be standing here today if it weren't for my dear family and friends."

Billy Bob goes down on one knee. Which makes it even harder to see him. "When my family used to gather at the old homestead, I'd stand on the front porch, just a-singing my heart out. I'd throw back my head and let loose:

"Oh Jedediah's donkey,

he's mean and he's spunky.

He'd go on down to the general store.

A bright red dress is what he wore."

Billy Bob sings a line or two. Badly.

"And my family would be a-sitting there, shelling peas, whittling wood, sharpening arrows. They would call out to me, 'Billy Bob, you stop singing now! Billy Bob, that is horrible, cut it out!' Or sometimes they would say 'You got this coming,' and they'd throw peas at me.

"With that kind of family love and support, why, any boy could dream of growing up to be the worst singer in America. So I decided to create a special event to bring families and friends together, the way my singing brought my family together."

"You're a good boy, Billy Bob," calls another voice.

"Why do they call him a boy when he's a big guy?" Bella asks a little too loudly.

"Maybe because he's silly?" Molly answers.

"Conor, we forgot to wave our sign," Jack whispers loudly enough for the whole store to hear.

"Wave it next time everyone cheers," I tell him.

"Good idea."

"Thank you, ma'am." Billy Bob tips his hat. "I knew I had to come back home and do something special for all of you!"

The crowd cheers. I pull Jack's sign out. He grabs one end. Timmy grabs the other. Jumping up and down, they yell, "Hey, Billy Bob!"

Since we're up front, he can't help but see them. He waves and reads their sign.

"Go, Billy Bob!" Jack yells.

Billy Bob goes all right. Goes white as a ghost. Grabs his throat and staggers backward. The room goes silent.

The lady with the tall yellow hair rushes over and pats his hand.

"What is the meaning of this?" asks Mr. G. Labanowski of the Doesn't That Smell Clean? Company.

Huh?

## Chapter Five

# And the Sign Says . . .

"It means we like him." Jack keeps jumping up and down.

"What's wrong with Billy Bob?" a voice calls out.

"Maybe he ate some bad candy?" Timmy suggests.

"What does that sign say?" someone asks.

"The sign says 'Ship's Cove Loves Billy Bob.'" Jack is loving all the attention. He turns to show the crowd.

Which goes silent for a moment. Till one voice says, "No, it don't."

Jack turns our way. We all read the words Jack didn't write:

"I ask you again, what is the meaning of this?" Mr. G. Labanowski doesn't look happy.

"I don't know, it's not my sign," Jack tells him.

"Whose sign is it?"

"I don't know. Conor gave it to me!" Jack announces loudly.

Everyone turns to me.

"I found it on the floor, and I thought it was Jack's," I tell Mr. Unhappy Green Shirt.

Billy Bob starts talking again. "Don't worry, don't worry. Just some kind of little ol' mistake. We don't let that kind of thing get us down, do we? No, we don't. Hoo-ah!" he yells.

"Hoo-ah!" most everyone yells back.

"Just what does that mean?" Mom asks.

"What are you trying to do? Get me in trouble?" Jack asks.

"I didn't do it, Jack." Why do I always end up saying those words whenever we solve a mystery? And boy, do we have a mystery to solve now.

"Now, where were we? Oh yes, my special event. Bringing family and friends together, that's what I'm fixing to do. And what better time than now? Halloween is just hiding around the corner? Isn't it? Am I right?"

"You're right, Billy Bob, you're right!"

"Candy, lots of candy!" Timmy yells.

"Now, you know what I'm talking about, don't you now?" Billy Bob points at all of us. "Halloween! That great day of people coming together, having fun, eating lots of candy. Pillowcases full! This is why I am pleased as punch to announce the First Annual Billy Bob Bidness Halloween Parade Costume Competition!"

The lady from the Doesn't That Smell Clean? Company starts clapping loudly.

Everyone else looks around. Halloween Parade?

"This is not going to be your any day ol' Halloween march around the school hall. No! No! Not some kind of awful parade that ends up with an unhappy little boy crying all by his lonesome in the corner. Some poor little boy who was all excited to be Superman. Who had a fancy red cape that trailed behind him. A cape that made him look good, make him look super. Till some big ol', mean ol' cousin of his steps on his Superman cape, rips it in half, and knocks the poor little boy to the ground, so that everyone laughs and the parade goes on without him. No, it won't be that kind of Halloween parade, will it?"

Billy Bob Bidness looks out at his audience. His audience looks back at him.

"Huh?" says Jack.

"He's telling some kind of story," Bella says.

Miss Evie Evans claps again.

Billy Bob stares at us.

The moment is kind of strange. Like his story.

Billy Bob shakes his head.

"Earth to Billy Bob, Earth to Billy Bob," Timmy says.

"Oh no," Billy Bob continues. "This is a parade, and a competition. One that will have families and friends working together for fun."

"Fun's good," Jack yells.

"This is good, son," Billy Bob promises. "Please listen, people, when I say that I would love to have everyone join in our parade. But the Lone Star State is one big state. So we had to choose a list of neighborhoods to join in the fun. But don't worry, if you're not on the list this year, you are sure to be next year. The fun will go on and on."

"Yay, Billy Bob!"

"So all you have to do is live in one of the neighborhoods on our list. Get together a team of ten people, with at least two grown-ups. Have a good ol' time creating a costume to wear together. For fun."

"And for fame, Billy Bob," Mr. G. Labanowski reminds him.

"That's right, pardners, for fame. The finals will be live on TV. Lights, camera, action! Everyone will be watching you compete. And watching me give you the prize. Now that is an exciting something." Billy Bob swings his hat over his head. "Hoo-ah!"

"Hoo-ah!" a lot of folks yell.

"TV! TV!" some others yell.

"Ten people? In one costume?" My mom looks as if she didn't hear him right.

"Okay, he's nuts," Molly McGuire says. "Let's go now."

"Go now?" Jack asks. "Who wants to go when we can be famous on television?"

"You're not going to get famous tonight, Jack. You have to enter the contest and win it."

"Okay, people. Now pick up a copy of the rules from the nice lady with the blue hair. And we will all have a wonderful, fun, happy time, as family, friends, and candy-eating Texans!" Billy Bob takes a bow as the crowd calls his name.

"With any luck, Ship's Cove won't be on the list," Mom tells Molly.

"No luck," Miz Barnes says. "You're on it."

"Ship's Cove Hula!" Timmy yells. But no one moves. There's no room.

"Ship's Cove going home," Mom announces.

I look around. Ship's Cove security guard already gone. The dogs are waiting, I guess.

"We have one week to tell them what our costume is," Jack reads from the rule sheet. "And one more week till the parade."

"That's not much time," Timmy says. "We'd better go home and start right away."

"We'd better go home and go to bed," Mom replies.

We'd better solve the mystery of the banners! Who made that other one? And what is the truth Billy Bob is supposed to tell?

## Chapter Six

# BUbba Loves Me, He Loves Me Not?

The next day at school, everyone talks about nothing but the contest. Who's on what team? What are they going to do? No, they can't tell you what they are going to do, it's a secret.

"It's a major emergency—we need to make a plan, Conor," Jack says at lunch. "There are going to be no grown-ups left on planet Earth to join our team."

"Are you going to eat that banana?" Timmy asks.

"And we need to solve the mystery," I remind them.

"Famous Jack on television first, mystery second."

"Tomorrow, The Secret Place, after school," I announce.

"Good banana," Timmy answers.

All alone, I head home from school. Jack has running practice, Timmy is helping in the school cafeteria, and Bella and Mugsy are off to some girls' club with uniforms.

Which means, yes! I will get to read Sir Chester. I'm thinking I know what that strange dragon is.

Bubba's truck turns the corner, heading my way. Lucy, the Vitalises' big dog, comes running out to the front lawn. I wonder how these dogs know that Bubba is coming. Is there a secret dog network? Little dog radios sending out news? "Bubba has turned off Buccaneer's Boulevard, heading toward The Lime in the Coconut Lane. Over and out."

Bubba moves slowly down the street. I wave. But Bubba doesn't wave back.

I guess he doesn't see me. He's probably got Lucy on his mind.

As he passes me, I hear loud music coming from his truck. What is that song? I know that song.

Lucy waits, tail waving like a flag. Till Bubba's truck gets really close. Then she holds up one paw in the air, like it hurts so bad. She tilts her head to the side, looking so sad.

Well, that'll be good for a few biscuits and a ride around the neighborhood.

Bubba pulls near Lucy's house. Bubba drives right on past Lucy's house. Drives right on past Lucy!

"Whoa!" I say out loud. Bubba's gone. And Lucy's still there.

Lucy runs inside. She's probably gone to send the warning: "Mayday! Mayday! Bubba drove past me! Ignored me! Did not stop to feed me!

Repeat, Bubba did not feed this dog. Mayday!"

I jog past the last few houses and scoot back to The Secret Place. Riley lies in the sun outside.

"Hey, big girl." I pet her on the run. She lifts her head, but doesn't get up. Probably too warm in the sun.

I pull Sir Chester from my backpack, then pull a big book from the shelf. Unfolding a long chart, I match a picture to the strange dragon.

"Aha," I say. "I was right." Bob the Hamster gives me a two-fist salute.

Now that I've uncovered the identity of the strange dragon, it's time to start working on the other mystery. I tape a large piece of paper to the wall. I write:

What truth is Billy Bob supposed
    to tell?
Who made the other poster and why?
Where is Jack's poster?

We'll work on these tomorrow after school. Now, I'll read at least three chapters of Sir Chester. But I can't help thinking I should write another question:

Why did Bubba drive past Lucy today? And what is that song he keeps playing?

"Conor, please! I want to do that!"

I step over Bella, who lies on the floor doing her famous imitation of a wooden board. A howling board.

"Bella, we've got to leave for school."

"Conor, you've got to say yes!"

I decide to explain one more time. "Bella, you can't be the grown-up in my group."

The wood begins to wail.

"Bella, it's because you're not a grown-up." This should be easy to understand.

"But I can pretend!"

"Bella, you have to *be* a real grown-up, pretending to be something else."

"Huh?" At least she's not wailing.

"I know. It's confusing. Why don't you just pretend you're happy and we can go to school?"

"Will that get me a prize?"

Timmy, Jack, and I walk to school with Bella, who is walking with Mugsy. Mugsy is my sister's best friend and, at five years old, a dangerous person.

Jack fires away. "Conor, what are we going to do? How are we going to do it? When are we going to do it? How can we win if we don't get going? Why aren't you answering my questions?"

"Because you haven't stopped for a second so I could," I explain. "The very first thing we have to do is find seven people to be on our team with us."

"No, we only need five more people. *And* two grown-ups," Jack corrects me.

"Who should be on our team?" Timmy asks.

"I'm thinking the three of us, and Murphy and Mad Dog," I suggest.

"That's five," Jack points out.

"I want to be the grown-up," Bella begins again. "Mugsy says I can do it."

"We'll need a lot of pink paint. And some fur. But I think it'll work," Mugsy says.

Pink paint?

"What is up with this?" Timmy asks as, a few hours later, we head into the playground for recess.

"This is just an outside guess. But I think a lot of the teams are way ahead of us," I tell them.

"But we've got to win!" Jack sounds worried.

Worried is probably a good idea.

The entire playground is filled with kids acting weird. But it definitely looks weird with a purpose.

"Look at them," Timmy points.

Jeremiah, Mick, Jake, and some other guys from the Sylvan Glen Sharks are trying to walk in a long line, each one really close to the guy in front. Except there is a big space in the middle. They move their arms and legs in slow motion. And fall down a lot.

"Caterpillar?" Timmy suggests.

"These are the Sylvan Glen Sharks," Jack reminds him.

"Oh, right." Timmy changes his mind. "Giant poisonous snake."

I'd have to agree with him. Except what's up with the hole in the middle?

"What are those guys doing?" Jack asks.

A group of, oh, about eight kids, mostly from Merrie Old England, are, well, sorta rolling around on the ground. And on top of one another. While holding on to one anothers' wrists and ankles.

"I have absolutely no idea," I answer truthfully.

"Whatever it is, it doesn't look good," Timmy says.

One group crawls across the grass on their stomachs, and some girls pile on top of one another in a pattern.

"Please get off my face," someone shouts.

"This isn't working," Jeremiah yells.

"It has to work. I want to be on TV."

"But it's not a good idea!"

"You have a better idea?"

"You're still standing on my face!"

"I can't understand you."

"That's because you're stepping on my face."

"AAARRRGGGHHH!"

"What was that noise?" Timmy asks.

"AAARRRGGGHHH!" Jack answers.

"No, not that noise." Timmy is on alert, sniffing the air.

"What?" I ask him.

"It's coming," Timmy says in a strange voice.

"Grocery Bag Boy is a little scary," Jack admits.

"I hear them," Timmy insists.

"Okay, scary."

"The bells, the bells." Timmy's eyes roll around a little.

"Okay, very scary."

"Wait, I hear them too," I tell Jack.

But it doesn't make sense.

The noise on the playground dies down, one kid at a time.

Soon, all we hear is the song.

"Ice cream!" someone yells.

Then another.

"Why is the ice-cream man coming?" Jack asks.

"Who cares why?" Timmy answers.

"Wait, that's not the Francisco's truck," I say. "Or is it?"

It's hard to tell. The truck is covered with big white sheets on both sides.

All I can see of the driver is a big cowboy hat

and a bandanna covering his face. Like the ones the bad guys wear when they rob a bank.

But I can see the words, the big blue words written on the white sheets.

Okay, there's definitely something going on around here.

## Chapter Seven

# Four Aliens Plus Four Kids Equals . . . ?

*Clang!*

"Conor, what're you doing? Are you working on our costume? What is our costume? Are we going to win? I want to win. And what did that sign on the truck mean today? Did you do it?"

Well, at least there's nothing funny going on with Jack. He's acting normal: slamming, pacing, snapping fingers, accusing me of being the bad guy.

"Hey hey, big guy," he says as he sticks his face up against Bob's hamster world. "You're glad to see me, aren't you?" Bob tries to scratch Jack's face through the glass.

"You're reading again, aren't you?" Jack accuses me.

"Good guess, Jack. What gave me away?" I ask. "Maybe the book in my hand?"

"How can you read at a time like this?" Jack throws his arms wide. "There's a chance to be on TV, be famous, and rich, and cool. But we aren't ready to be in the contest. Look, even Riley's worried. She isn't jumping around, or anything."

Riley opens one eye when Jack says her name. She's quiet today, if I think about it. I wonder . . .

*Clang!*

Timmy falls into the room.

"Okay, here's the deal," he says. He's reading from a candy bar wrapper while he's still in a forward roll.

Impressive.

"Mad Dog is taken; so are Brendan and Josh. Mr. Lefty has agreed to be one of the grown-ups for Merrie Old England. The other one is the Howler." Timmy pauses to breathe.

"The Howler!" Jack and I say at the same time.

"Poor Mr. Lefty," Timmy agrees. The Howler is Gavin's mom, who earned her name from how she watches roller hockey games.

Timmy checks his notes. "Coach Maggie is helping the Maniac Maccabees. Miss Karen won't say what she is doing, but I heard Rachel Zummo, Lily, and other girls in her office singing about a road."

"This is not good," Jack says.

"Why, what've we got?" Timmy asks.

"You're looking at it." Jack sighs.

"When does the entry form have to be in?" Timmy asks.

"Tomorrow," I tell them.

"We're doomed, doomed." Jack falls to the floor.

"All we have to do is turn in our form." I explain the rules again. "It has to say who's on our team, with a picture or drawing of the costume. You don't make the costume till you're a finalist."

"But we don't know who's on our team or

what our costume is," Timmy reminds me.

"And how do we put in a picture if we don't have the costume?" Jack has a point. This is never a good sign.

"We'll figure something out," I promise. "Murphy's on the way over. She'll be on our team."

"Still need six more people." Timmy holds up six fingers.

"What we need is a wild idea," I suggest.

"Something really wild," Jack agrees.

"Something just like that!" Timmy shouts, pointing to the window.

Jack leaps to his feet. He screams, "NO!"

I have to admit that's too wild, even for me.

The horrible faces of space creatures fill the window, blocking even the sight of the sky. They stare at us. Make faces at us. Shake their horrible heads at us. We stand still, frozen with shock, until we hear . . .

*Clang.*

Murphy bangs into the room. "Sorry! I had to bring them with me. I promised to watch Mikey. And they were already like that."

"Do they have any rope?" Jack asks in a trembling voice.

"We'll protect you, Jack," I promise.

"We will?" Timmy asks.

"Come on in, all of you," I call to the four purple-faced, green-armed, foil-headed creatures.

"Smargdfph!" they all shout at me.

"It was all Mugsy's idea," Bella says. I had figured this out already.

"I scared myself," Dwayne tells Timmy.

"Here you go, big buddy, this will help." Timmy gives him something silver to eat. Which matches his hair. Which, like the other kids' hair, sticks straight up in the air because it's wrapped in lots and lots of aluminum foil.

"We're going to win the contest," Mugsy says. "Just as soon as someone can write out the paper for us."

"But you need more people. And grown-ups," I tell her. "And you're supposed to be one costume with everyone in it."

"Okay, you fix it," Mugsy orders.

"Please, please, please, Conor? Let us be in the parade with you." Bella pulls on my little finger and gives me the Sad Little Sister face. Which is so not fair, since I taught her that trick.

"Great idea," Timmy says. "Look, now there are eight of us."

"We would only need two more," Murphy points out.

"Conor," Jack whispers in my ear, "we can't do this. Mugsy is dangerous. And Dwayne is, he's, you know, Dwayne."

Jack is right. But so is Timmy. And the hour is late.

"Jack, with these kids, we can go all the way! Billy Bob wants family? We've got family here. He wants friends? We've got lots of friends. He wants fun? This is a funny crowd!" I'm rolling now. "It'll be lights, camera, action! Television!"

"Movie stars!" Bella yells.

"I'm the evil ninja warrior queen!" Mugsy shows off her action moves.

Jack hides behind Dwayne.

Bob the Hamster copies Mugsy.

Riley rolls over on her back and sighs. What's wrong with her?

"We'll have our pictures on candy bars!" Timmy shouts.

"Now we have to find us some grown-ups," I remind them.

"Mom!" says Bella.

"Bubba!" says Timmy.

## Chapter Eight

# Secret Mission: Find Bubba

My mission: to ride around the neighborhood and find Bubba.

Bella's mission: to make the sad face at Mom till she agrees to do it.

Murphy, Jack, and Timmy's mission: to keep the other three aliens from destroying anything. Or anyone.

I pass Maeve, the big wolfhound, lying on her

lawn, looking sad.

And Maximillian, the collie, sitting with one paw up in the air.

Riley's pal Smidgen lies on a doggie bench in front of her house. She is wearing an orange outfit decorated with leaves. She doesn't bark at me. Nellie the greyhound doesn't race along her fence when I go by. When Clara, the runaway beagle, sees me, she doesn't even halloo. My keen detective skills tell me something is not right with the dogs of Ship's Cove.

Well, there's one person who would know, and I'm looking for him.

And I'm seeing him.

Bubba's truck turns into Ship's Cove Cove. This should shortly bring him around to Dinghy Drive. As I race to catch him, I see Smidgen turn in to Dinghy, dragging her back leg.

No need to rush now. That limp is good for serious dog biscuits.

But Bubba's truck comes around the corner without stopping. I break into warp-speed riding to catch him. As I pass Smidgen, she is lying on her back kicking her paws up and down.

I didn't know dogs could throw tantrums.

"Hey hey, Bubba," I call when I find his truck parked by the rowboat. "Can I talk to you?"

Bubba turns down the loud music. What is that song he keeps playing? "I have to get back on patrol," he says.

"How about I ask fast?" I practiced asking nicely before I came over.

Bubba listens. And answers fast.

"Bubba said what?" my mom asks as she stands dripping pink and red paint onto the floor of The Secret Place.

"He said, 'It wouldn't be right.' And he said his daddy always told him, 'Don't fib, do what's right, and be the best you that you can be.' And then he took his hat off and put it over his heart."

"Funny," Timmy says.

"What's funny is he didn't stop to visit one dog," I tell everyone. "He drove past Smidgen when Smidgen was pretending to limp."

"Smidgen? But he's Smidgen's uncle Bubba," Timmy says, which we all know.

"That doesn't sound like Bubba," Molly McGuire says.

"Something's wrong," I declare. *Great, another mystery,* I think.

"But it doesn't matter," Murphy points out. "We have two grown-ups now."

"Who?" I ask.

"Me, plus your mom, is two," Molly answers.

"Mom, you'll do it?"

"How could I turn down such a perfect team?" she answers.

I look at four space aliens: Jack, who's shadow-boxing with Bob; Timmy, who's eating a dog biscuit with Riley; and Murphy.

A perfect team?

"We need to decide on a costume, pronto," Molly announces.

"I'll draw the picture for the entry form tonight," Mom adds.

"Costume! Costume!" Timmy starts the chant.

"This should be easy," Jack says.

One hour later, the large white sheets of paper labeled COSTUME IDEAS are covered with words:

1) The major organs of the body
2) Santa's reindeer
3) A big box of candy
4) Hockey skates
5) Food
6) An alien spaceship

7) Unicorns
8) A race car

"You know, I just don't feel the right one is there," my mom says.

"Anyone would want to be a box of candy," Timmy replies. "And Billy Bob loves candy."

"But he's not the only judge," Molly points out.

"We need something that comes in all sizes," Mom says. "Something that runs, you know, big to small."

"Candy does," Timmy insists.

Big to small? Why does that sound so familiar? Big to small. No! Small to big!

"I think I have it," I tell everyone. I quickly look through my books till I find the right one.

I show them the chart I found yesterday.

"Very cool," Timmy says.

"Could we do that?" Jack asks.

"We can do that," my mom says, "working in costume overdrive."

"Overdrive! Land speed records! That's what we detectives are all about," Jack promises.

"I think we've got it," Molly says.

"What do you say, little aliens?" Timmy asks as he holds up the picture.

"I think I'll scare myself," Dwayne says.

"I think I ate something like that once," Mikey says, pointing to the smallest one.

"Great," Murphy says.

"I am going to be this one." Mugsy points.

"But that's not a little one," Bella explains.

"But it is so Mugsy," my mom says.

And she is so right.

"Hoo-ah, we have a plan!" Timmy says.

Thank you, Sir Chester's Strange Dragons.

## Chapter Nine

# Conor Does It Again

"Now that is a seriously scary sight," Jack announces as our whole team stands looking in the window of the Big Blue Bookstore. Glowing skeletons shake their bones, tombstones open and close, spiders climb up and down the window. Miz Barnes has great books and great windows.

"Does it remind you of your family?" Timmy asks.

"Ho, ho. Joke Boy strikes again," Jack answers.

"Actually, you have the wrong holiday. It's Halloween, not Christmas, Ho Ho Boy."

"Actually, it's National Beat Your Friend at Wrestling Day," Jack tells him. He starts to go for Timmy.

"Actually, it's Do Exactly What Conor's Mother

Says at All Times Day." Mom grabs both of them. "Which is to stand here nicely till we're done."

A smaller crowd than the last one is gathered outside the Big Blue Bookstore. But everyone here is hoping Billy Bob Bidness will choose his or her team to march in his Halloween parade. And there's a guy with a TV camera, and a few photographers.

"I heard there were thirty entries," Molly said. "And they'll pick five."

"Here they come," Jack says.

"Howdy, howdy, howdy!" Billy Bob calls as he comes out of the store. "It's a great day to be together. I have to start out by saying, there are some crazy good ideas in all your heads. If we didn't pick you, don't go playing sad songs on the jukebox. We thought your idea was great, we really did."

"There are five finalists," Miz Barnes tells us.

"Billy Bob'll announce the name of the neighborhood, and the name of the team. I'll post the list of winners on the door, so everyone can see."

"Hold on to your great big hats, here we go." Billy Bob unfolds a piece of paper.

"The first finalist is the Somewhere Over the Prairie team from the Painted Desert."

Screams and shouts from Miss Karen, Rachel, Lily, and the other girls.

"The number two spot goes to the Take Me Out to the Ball Game team from Merrie Old England."

"YES!" screams the Howler.

"Now we have Sylvan Glen's entry: I Can't Believe I Ate the Whole Thing."

"Sharks rule," Jake yells.

"Greetings, Earthlings, the entry from Pie Town, is a winner."

A photographer takes a picture of that team.

"And last, but not least, the Strange Dragons of

Ship's Cove are finalists." Billy Bob folds his paper.

"Hoo-ah!" Timmy and Jack shout at the same time.

Bella and Mugsy do cartwheels. Dwayne tries, but he falls on his head.

"Strange Dragon dance," Timmy calls. Most of our team joins in. Me, I'm watching Billy Bob. I can't help wondering what truth he's supposed to tell. And who wants him to do it?

"Conor, give me a hand." Miz Barnes waves the piece of paper at me. "Unroll it slowly while I attach the top."

"Let's get a picture for the paper," a lady with a camera says. "Billy Bob, stand closer, please?"

Billy Bob moves in and smiles. Miz Barnes holds the top, smiling. Turning toward the camera, I unroll slowly.

"Uh-oh," Mom says loudly.

"Hey, get a picture of that," someone else yells. We all turn to read the words.

"Conor, you did it again," Jack shouts.

## Chapter Ten

# Heigh Ho, Heigh Ho

The Secret Place is no longer the home of a top crime-fighting group, ready at any minute to do good and solve mysteries. No, our all-important headquarters is now Costume Central.

My mom and Timmy work two sewing machines at one end of the room. I feel this is not a good influence on Bob. He appears to be doing aerobics along with the machine.

On a long piece of paper, the rest of us paint a scene outlined in pencil. Oh, and try on our costumes.

"With these arms on, I can't eat," Timmy says, worried.

"You will only have them on for the parade," Molly reminds him.

"See, that's a problem," Timmy says.

Riley does nothing. The Beast just lies in the middle of the mess.

I think about the other mess. Which would be the picture of me on the front page of the paper. Holding up the banner urging

Billy Bob to tell the truth.

LOCAL YOUTH BOTHERS FAMOUS TV STAR.

That's the headline. The story uses a lot of words to say something short: I didn't do it.

But who did? That's the big question on top of another question: What do the signs mean?

And what's wrong with Bubba anyway? And what's that song he keeps playing? And . . . and . . .

"All right! The crucial moment is upon us," Mom says in a Very Important voice. "Ladies and Gentlemen, don your costumes."

It takes a little while to get organized. Mikey has Bella's arms. Murphy swears that Timmy's head is her head. But Molly has a diagram for each costume.

"Whoa!" Jack shouts when we're all finished.

"Big whoa!" Murphy adds.

"Is it us?" Dwayne asks in a small voice.

"Line up," Molly orders. "You should know where you stand. No, Mugsy, you can't go there, you didn't exist yet."

"I know, I know. I just wanted to pretend I was eating Mikey," she says.

Molly marches up and down the line. She straightens a head, adjusts a back, moves an eyeball.

"Way good," she says. "Now, parade, turn right."

We do. Though some of us take more than one try.

"Awesome," says Molly. "I believe we are good to go."

"Is it time to eat yet?" Timmy asks.

"I'll eat Dwayne," Mugsy growls.

"It's time for pizza at Speed's," Mom announces.

"Pizza! Pizza!" everyone shouts.

"We have to drop the costumes off at Big Blue," she adds. "So we can do it all at one time."

"Pizza! Pizza!" we still shout.

"We're not going anywhere," Molly growls at us, "till everyone puts his or her head in a bag."

We load the costumes in big black garbage bags. After piling them into Mom's and Molly's cars, we head to Big Blue.

"Are you guys good to go?" Miz Barnes asks.

"Good to go," we tell her.

"Good luck," Miz Barnes says. "And smile for the cameras. Except maybe you, Conor."

"Conor's a famous bad guy," Jack singsongs.

"Freaky Joe's Rule Number Sixteen: A Club Member Is Always Loyal. Remember that, Jack." My mom looks big-time serious at him. "Clear?"

"Clear," Jack answers.

"Good. Now pizza, which can fix anything."

"Oh, Speed's. I'm coming." Timmy walks out of the store, his nose in the air.

Everything at Speed's is always just the same: red and white tablecloths, and a big statue of a man who is singing and holding a pizza. The statue looks like Mr. Speed.

So here we are, eating great pizza and talking about how we are going to wear our costumes, walk in them, and carry the painting.

Then Jack shouts, "Look!"

Billy Bob Bidness fills up one half of the screen on the big TV set mounted on the wall behind the counter. I fill up the other.

"No, I'm not worried about those signs," Billy Bob tells the newswoman. "I am having me a good ol' Texas good time, and I can't wait till the parade."

I try to quietly slide under the table.

"Besides, my uncle Shep, he always told me to do the right thing and to be the best me I can. I'm sure that young'un's folks will tell him the same."

What did he say?

"You're not worried about another sign ruining your parade?" The reporter holds the microphone closer.

"I'm not worried; I'm not worried one little bit. To show you, I'll sing a little of my song."

Billy Bob sings a bit about Chuck.

"Billy Bob sounded funny there," Bella says.

"I want to be like Conor when I grow up," Mugsy says.

## Chapter Eleven

# Please Call B-U-B-B-A

I need to talk to someone, I realize. And I say so out loud.

"I know you do, sweetie," Mom says. "Let's get these kids home. . . ."

"I need to *go* talk to someone," I explain. "It's big-time important. Rule One-D."

"'If There's Something Important to Do, Then Do It,'" Mom quotes.

"Exactly," I answer.

"We're outta here," she tells me. "What is that you have?" she asks Mugsy.

Who is attacking the man making the pizzas.

"It's one of my hands," she admits.

"Everything is supposed to be in your costume bag," Molly says in a not-so-happy voice.

"But I love it so," Mugsy tells her.

"Come on, Valerie gave me a key. We'll drop it off at the store on the way home."

"Wait in the car," Mom tells the crowd of us. "Don't leave the vehicle. Don't. Mugsy, you can only breathe."

Bella, Murphy, and Mikey wave to us from Molly's car.

Mom doesn't come out right away. Through the window I can see her

roaming. This doesn't seem the time to look for something new to read.

She finally comes out, looking worried. I roll down my window to hear what she's saying to Molly.

"Molly, they're not there."

Molly jumps out of the car. "We left them in the back corner."

"Which is where they are not now."

"Call Valerie," Molly insists.

"I did. She says she didn't touch them after we left."

Molly marches into the store.

I've got a bad feeling about this.

She marches out. "What are we going to do?" she asks Mom.

"Something terrible to the person who took them." Mom has a real and true mad on. "Valerie is on her way here."

We all pile into the store to wait for Miz Barnes.

"This should be cool and exciting," Jack says.

"But it's not," Timmy admits.

"Who would want to do something terrible to us?" Murphy asks.

"I think I'm going to cry, Conor," Bella says.

"Someone is going down," Mugsy declares.

Mikey and Dwayne hide under the table.

"I think we should call Bubba," Bella says.

"How will that help?" Jack asks. "He's just driving around in his truck these days, ignoring dogs, playing the same ol' song over and over."

Bingo.

Yes! I am right.

"I have to go home, Mom."

"Sweetie, I have to wait here for Valerie," Mom says.

"Could Molly drive me? Please? I have to talk to that someone." I give her the Please, Do This for Me look.

She gives me the Thinking Mom look back.

"Deal. Molly will drive you home and wait with you until he shows up."

"Yes!"

"Where's Conor going?" Bella asks as I jump into Molly's car.

To save the day! I hope.

## Chapter Twelve

# Fibbing Is Just Fibbing

"You really and truly think this is a good idea?" Molly asks me for the 432nd time.

"I do."

"The parade is tomorrow," she reminds me. For the 433rd time.

"I know. I have a good feeling about this."

"Freaky Joe's Rule Number Twenty-Two?" she asks.

"Exactly."

"Well, it worked for me once. See you soon."

Rule Twenty-Two: If You Think You're Right, You Might Be.

The Ship's Cove Security truck arrives. Clipboard in hand, pencil dangling from a piece of string,

Bubba walks over to where I wait in front of the house.

"Your momma called. You have a big problem?" Bubba asks.

"A major, awful, disastrous problem," I say.

"Hang on, I'm still writing *big*," Bubba says, licking the pencil again.

"Bubba," I tell him, "it has to do with Billy Bob Bidness."

Bubba stops writing. He sits down on the back bumper of the truck. "I'm listening."

I sit next to him. "It's about his parade. You know, tomorrow?"

"Yup."

"Someone took our costumes from the bookstore. We worked

hard. Timmy did a lot of sewing. And now they're gone."

"Gone?" Bubba chews the pencil. Kicks the street. Has on a big, hard-thinking face.

"Can I ask you a question?"

"I guess I don't mind."

"What were you wearing when Superman lost his cape?" I ask.

"I was a cowboy," he answers. "And it was an accident."

"Had to be," I agree.

He stops.

"How did you know?" Bubba asks me.

"Two things: I finally recognized the song you keep playing. It sounds so good."

"It's swell," Bubba says. "What's the other?"

"Something your daddy said." And I tell him.

"Taking costumes is different from fibbing." Bubba looks really unhappy.

"The best thing is to get them back," I tell him.

Bubba stands up. "You'll have them by the morning," he promises.

"You can get them? For sure?" I ask.

"I know something that will get them back. And I could tell."

"Thanks, Bubba," I tell him.

"Big Bubba is on the job. My daddy said if something is broke, then fix it."

"He had good ideas," I tell Bubba.

"I've been driving around thinking hard about them since I first saw that show," Bubba says.

"Thinking real hard always makes me forget other stuff I gotta do," I tell Bubba.

"Huh?" Bubba looks at me funny.

"Lot of sad faces around here," I tell him.

"I got something to do first." Bubba hops in his truck.

"It'll be okay," I say to Mom a little while later.

"He'll come," I say to Riley when we sneak outside in the early morning.

"I'll help you with those," I say to Bubba when he comes in the door of The Secret Place with the first two bags.

"Well, look who's here. Who's a big girl?" Bubba asks Riley when all ten bags are present and accounted for. "What have you been doing with yourself? Have you been too busy to see your uncle Bubba? Do you need a treat, big girl? How about a ride?"

Riley looks like someone told her Christmas was canceled for good and then Santa showed up on the front doorstep.

"Oh, you need two treats?" Bubba asks. "Who's so smart? Okay, then, let's go out to the truck."

"Bubba?" I say.

"What, big fella?"

"Thank you," I say, pointing at the bags.

"Weren't nothing to it. I finally decided everyone fibs now and again, even if it's not right. I just have to let that go. Besides," Bubba says, "I have more important things to do than worry about that all day."

Riley lies on her back, moaning.

"Riley and I've got some business to do," Bubba says. "And I think you'd better remember, there're some big doings later today."

## Chapter Thirteen

# Do Aliens Wear Tap Shoes?

Big doings is right.

"Ship's Cove, thank goodness you're here." Miss Evie Evan races over to us. "You're to get ready in Big Corral Number Three. Follow me."

We carry our bags and scenery over to some hay bales, which are piled up person-high, with a curtain for a door. Bright lights are everywhere, and there are people with headphones and cameras.

"Oh boy," Mugsy says. Molly grabs her.

Miss Evans hands us a pile of paper. "You're the last entry in the parade. Someone will come for you and lead you right to where you need to be."

"Can we see the parade?" Timmy asks.

"Over there," Miss Evan points. "Just stay off camera till your time."

"This is officially time to get dressed!" Mom announces.

"Let's go over the song one last time," Molly suggests.

We chant. We know the words.

"We are good to go," Mom says. "I'll carry the scenery till we start."

"Let's go watch," Timmy says.

"Only if at least six people hold on to Mugsy at all times," Molly says.

People are everywhere, standing, sitting on bleachers or on cars, even standing on trucks.

"I never wanted to be on TV," Jack says.

"Good time to bring it up," Timmy tells him.

"Look, Bubba came." Bella points.

Bubba and his truck have found a place along the parade route. The truck is filled with happy-looking dogs who are all wearing orange pumpkin hats on their heads. Bubba has one on as well.

"Ladies and Gentlemen and Texans of all ages! Let's give a big warm welcome to Mr. Billy Bob Bidness," says Mr. G. Labanowski, president of the Doesn't That Smell Clean? Company.

Billy Bob, in his biggest hat and fanciest shirt, runs up onto a big stage set at the head of the parade.

"Hoo-ah," Billy Bob says. "What a night! I know what you all came for, so let's not waste time talking about how good I look, and start the parade."

"And remember, a trophy and a year's supply of cleaning products go to the winner!" says Mr. G. Labanowski.

"How about that?" yells Billy Bob. "Now on with the show!"

Music that sounds like it would come from a circus fills the air.

"Our first contestants, representing the Painted

Desert, call their costume Somewhere Over the Prairie."

All the girls are dressed in gold, with big, strange square things strapped to their heads. Which turn out to be gold brick squares. As they march forward, squeezing close together, the squares fit together to make a yellow brick road. They tap-dance as they sing "Follow, follow, follow."

Miss Karen, dressed like a good witch, and Miss Martha, dressed like a bad one, boogie along beside them. The audience sings and claps along.

"I like that green-faced lady," Mugsy says.

"Give them a big hand," Billy Bob says. "And keep it going for the crew from Merrie Old England and Take Me Out to the Ball Game."

Mr. Lefty, dressed like a baseball player, carries a funny, giant bat. The Howler is an umpire. The

kids are dressed all in white with white stuff covering their heads.

"Batter up!" the Howler howls.

The kids some-how huddle together and make the ball.

"Very cool," Jack says.

Mr. Lefty takes a big swing with the bat. And connects with the ball. Which rolls off down the parade route.

Everyone begins to sing "Take Me Out to the Ball Game."

The dogs bark along loudly, in tune.

"Isn't this a wonderful time?" Billy Bob shouts.

"Coming at you is I Can't Believe I Ate the Whole Thing from the folks in Sylvan Glen."

Our guess was good. A giant, poisonous snake slithers out. Everyone manages to move slowly and together. But this poisonous snake recently swallowed something really big. The middle of the snake bulges big and wide. The bulge is filled with Big Buster and his brother Kenny.

"A snake like that can open its jaw eight times wider than its body," I tell my team. I learned this from *The Big Book of Reptiles*.

"Don't get scared now, but here comes

Greetings, Earthlings from Pie Town."

The alien invaders are ready to go. They carry a spaceship covered with signs: GIVE US YOUR COOKIES and EARTHLINGS, WE WANT YOUR BUBBLE GUM.

"Evil aliens," Timmy says.

We're next.

"Heads on, claws in position?" Drill Sergeant Molly checks us out.

"Everyone in the right order?"

"Unrolling scroll." Timmy takes the handle at one end.

I walk the other end all the way back and hand it to Jack and Mugsy.

Billy Bob leads the crowd in some song about flying purple aliens.

"Ship's Cove rocks," Mom says.

"Our last entry," Billy Bob tells everyone, "is the Strange Dragons of Ship's Cove!"

## Chapter Fourteen

# Billy Bob Tells the Truth

"Wait for the count," Molly says. "Sing it loud, sing it proud."

We don't need Billy Bob to find a song for us.

"One and two," Molly says, setting the beat, "and now we go."

"We don't know but we've been told,
Dinosaurs are mighty bold.
Once upon this earth, our home,
We did wander, we did roam.
Give it up, two, three, four,
Give a roar, two, three, four."

We roar. We thud along, carrying our scenery with us. The giant scroll says THE AGE OF THE DINOSAURS. It is painted from one end to the other with the forests, lakes, flowers, and volcanoes from the places where dinosaurs roamed.

Above Timmy, Murphy, and Dwayne are the words TRIASSIC PERIOD. They sing two lines each, in order:

> "You can call me Plateosaur.
> I'll step on your foot, and you'll be sore."
> "I am called Coelophysis.
> Me, you just don't want to kiss."
> "A dinosaur the size of a cat,
> I'm Saltopus, imagine that."
> "Give it up, two, three, four.
> Give a roar, two, three, four."

We all join in for the last two lines, and Mom, Bella, Mikey, and I do the same thing for JURAS-SIC PERIOD.

> "Apatasaurus, that's my name.
> I'm one giant, gentle dame."

"Xiaosaurus, so tall I stand,
Ancient China is my land."
"I got big teeth and I got big claw,
Allosaurus like to eat the dinosaur."
"Compsognathus, Compsognathus.
I am small but I am kicking.
A dinosaur the size of a chicken."
"Give it up, two, three, four.
Hear us roar, two, three, four."

Way cool. The crowd joins us on the last line. The Age of the Dinosaurs moves on down the parade route. The Cretaceous Period—Molly, Jack, and Mugsy—begins to sing.

"On my head you better not hop;
You'll find the three horns of Triceratop."
"Who's so fast, he'll win, he'll score?
Speed man, me, Velociraptor."
"Look at me, I'm so big, I'm so mean,

Tyrannosaurus Rex, king of this scene."

Mugsy roars louder than anyone.

"Give it up, two, three, four.
Hear us roar, two, three, four."

The crowd chants with us.

We're coming to the end of the parade. I can see the other teams waiting ahead of us.

I can hear a funny noise somewhere near us.

"Roar. Roar. I'm hungry; I can eat some more," Mugsy is still singing, making up words as she goes.

I hear, "Grrr. Grrr."

I hear Bubba yell, "No, Smidgen! These are good dinosaurs."

Smidgen runs over to us, growling as loud as a teeny dog can growl.

"No, doggie, don't bite my claw," Bella yells. Smidgen is shaking Bella's foot. Which makes it hard for her to thud along.

Bubba yells, "Riley, stay in the truck!"

But Riley heard Bella's unhappy voice. She bounds out of the truck, jumping and sniffing, looking for Bella.

I come to a complete stop.

The Cretaceous Era keeps going.

"Watch out," the Velociraptor yells. As he falls into Triceratops.

"Tyrannosaurus loves to eat Triceratops!" Mugsy leaps on top of both of them.

"Cut that out," Jack yells.

Riley knows that voice. She jumps on the pile.

The other dogs come over to check us out.

They run around checking the other teams out.

Smidgen has stopped eating the Xiaosaurus and attacks the alien ship.

Mom takes her head off.

"This is not good," she says, looking around.

"You think?" I say as Mugsy starts chasing Mikey and Dwayne. And Nellie the greyhound and Maeve the wolfhound chase the yellow brick road.

The crowd cheers.

"What is going on back there?" Billy Bob calls out. "Have we got an itty-bitty little problem?"

Triceratops, Apatosaurus, and Allosaurus try to catch the dogs.

"What in tarnation?" Billy Bob comes flying back to where we are. Followed by two men with TV cameras.

He runs into me as I corral Riley. Bubba puts Sally in the truck. Smidgen hangs off Mom's costume, growling.

"How?" Billy Bob begins. "What?" he says, looking around. "Who?" he shouts.

"Conor," Jack begins.

"Shush," Mom says.

"It's okay, baby," Bubba says, picking up Maeve. Who is taller than Bubba.

"You!" Billy Bob shouts. "I should have known it was you."

"Now, calm down a minute," Bubba begins.

"I will not calm down." Billy Bob points at Bubba. "This man has brought these dogs here tonight for the single purpose of ruining this parade."

Billy Bob notices the camera. He looks right up close. "That's right, America, this man likes to ruin parades."

Bubba puts Maeve down. "Billy Bob, you just gotta stop this. One time, your cousin Bubba was not paying attention in school. Because he looked out the window and saw a little puppy dog sitting by the school door. So he didn't notice that the costume parade stopped. So he stepped on his little cousin's cape just as the little cousin started to walk. All of this was a long time ago."

Billy Bob keeps talking to the camera. "This man is a parade-ruining bad guy."

"Bubba is not a bad guy!" I shout. "He's a great guy. And a friend to dogs everywhere." I realize I'm saying this last bit with a camera in my face.

"Thanks, ol' buddy," Bubba says. He whistles. "Doggies, come. Treats for everyone."

Dogs come flying.

"Parade ruiner, parade ruiner," Billy Bob chants.

Miss Evie Evans and Mr. G. Labanowski come running.

"We are live, Billy Bob," they tell him.

"Good. All of Texas—all of America—can see what a bad guy looks like." Billy Bob points at Bubba.

Smidgen doesn't like the way he's talking.

She leaps out of the truck. Growling, she grabs one of Billy Bob's big boots.

"Stupid little mutt," Billy Bob says.

"Don't call the dog stupid," Bubba says. "Come here, baby, come away from the mean man."

"I'm mean?" Billy Bob says.

"And you're a fibber, too," Bubba says. "Tell the truth, Billy Bob."

"A fibber?" Billy Bob shouts.

Mr. G. Labanowski has turned the cameras over to where he stands.

"And we hope you enjoyed this fun-filled, madcap Halloween parade. And that you will all tune in this winter for the second round of *Did You Hear That?*, when we once again search for the worst singer in America."

"What?" Billy Bob turns away from Bubba.

"I think it's time we said thank you and good night from lovely Houston."

"Tarnation, how can you find the worst singer in America, if you already did find him, and it was me?" Billy Bob interrupts.

"We'll find another." Mr. G. Labanowski doesn't look happy.

"You can't have two worst. Either I am or I ain't," Billy Bob declares. "Are you going to give him a parade as well?"

"Him or her," Miss Evie Evans points out.

"Well, I'll be a ding dang dong," Billy Bob says. He turns to the crowd. "What do you think of these folks, huh? You can tell they're not true Texans. They promise a body fame and fortune if he comes on their show and is the worst singer there is. But they don't tell you that it's just till they find another one."

Billy Bob throws his cowboy hat down on the ground. "That man may be a parade ruiner, but you guys are worse. To think that I worked so hard to sing that bad for you. Especially . . ."

"Especially what?" Mr. G. Labanowski looks confused.

"Tell the truth, Billy Bob," Bubba yells.

"Tell the truth, Billy Bob," someone in the crowd yells.

Billy Bob tells the truth. "Especially when I have a voice like an angel. That's what my family always told me when we were sitting around our apartment in the city. Like an angel."

"We made tapes, he was so good," Bubba says. "Listen."

Bubba reaches inside his truck and turns the music he's been playing up really loud.

"Whoa," says the crowd.

"I got a voice as beautiful as Texas," Billy Bob says.

"As beautiful as Texas," Bubba says, wiping a tear from his eye.

"Sing us one, Billy Bob," someone yells.

"The stars at night are big and bright,
deep in the heart of Texas."

He sings it well.

We all sing along. Even Bubba and his dogs.

## Chapter Fifteen

# That's the End Again

The Secret Place is filled with secret agents, and little sisters, and little sisters' friends—all the kids from the Age of the Dinosaurs.

"These dinosaur cookies are great!" Timmy says as he shares one with Riley.

"It was nice of the Doesn't That Smell Clean? Company to send them." Jack eats two at one time.

"Well, they couldn't really declare a winner, since Billy Bob never got to judge," I explain. They are good cookies.

"How come you're not a famous bad guy?" Mugsy asks in a disappointed voice.

"'Cause I didn't write those signs," I explain again. "Bubba did. He slipped one under my chair in the bookstore. And he talked Pablo into switching the other one. Pablo thought it was a joke."

"Miz Barnes didn't think it was funny," Timmy points out.

"But her store is famous now, so that's okay," I remind them.

"And how did you figure out that Bubba's daddy was Billy Bob's uncle?" Jack is still sore at me for solving the mystery.

"Bubba and Billy Bob used the same words to say something Bubba's daddy and Billy Bob's uncle said. And I knew there had to be a connection because of the way Bubba was acting. When I realized the song Bubba was playing was Billy Bob's, I had it. It just took me so long because it's hard to recognize Billy Bob when he's not fake-singing."

"I've decided I'm going to enter the next competition," Timmy announces. "I'm working on my song now."

"Don't," Bella says.

"Candy candy, it's fine and dandy. I like it clean and I like it sandy!"

"That's really bad." Dwayne covers his ears.

"See!" Timmy shouts.

"See what? See me attack the bad singer?" Jack tackles Timmy. Riley tackles Jack. Bella and Mugsy tackle Riley. Mikey and Dwayne jump around and around.

Just another day in the life of the Freaky Joe Club.

I pick up Sir Chester the Clever. Chuck is about to explain what a dinosaur is.

There's nothing like a good mystery to pass the time.

I duck as Jack's shoe flies by.

Want things to start going your way?

Don't forget to read the next adventure of

# The Freaky Joe Club

## Secret File #6:

### The Case of the Singing SeaDragons

# The Freaky Joe Club

Meet Conor, Jack, and Timmy, the members (along with The Beast) of the latest chapter of the Freaky Joe Club. Join them as they solve crimes and fight evil in Ship's Cove, Texas. Watch them conquer the bullies from Sylvan Glen. And mo important, help them figure out:

## WHO IS FREAKY JOE?!?!?

Coming soon:
**SECRET FILE #6:
THE CASE OF THE
SINGING
SEADRAGONS**

Aladdin Paperbacks • Simon & Schuster Children's Division